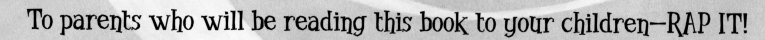
To parents who will be reading this book to your children—RAP IT!

Get out of your seat!
Get up on your feet!
Turn up the heat!
Give me a beat!
I repeat!

Give me a beat!

RAPPY GOES TO SCHOOL

To Nina, Sam, and Emma
—D.G.

To my friend Kay Petryszak
—T.B.

The artist used Adobe Illustrator to create the digital illustrations for this book.
Typography by Rick Farley
16 17 18 19 20 SCP 10 9 8 7 6 5 4 3 2 1
❖
First Edition

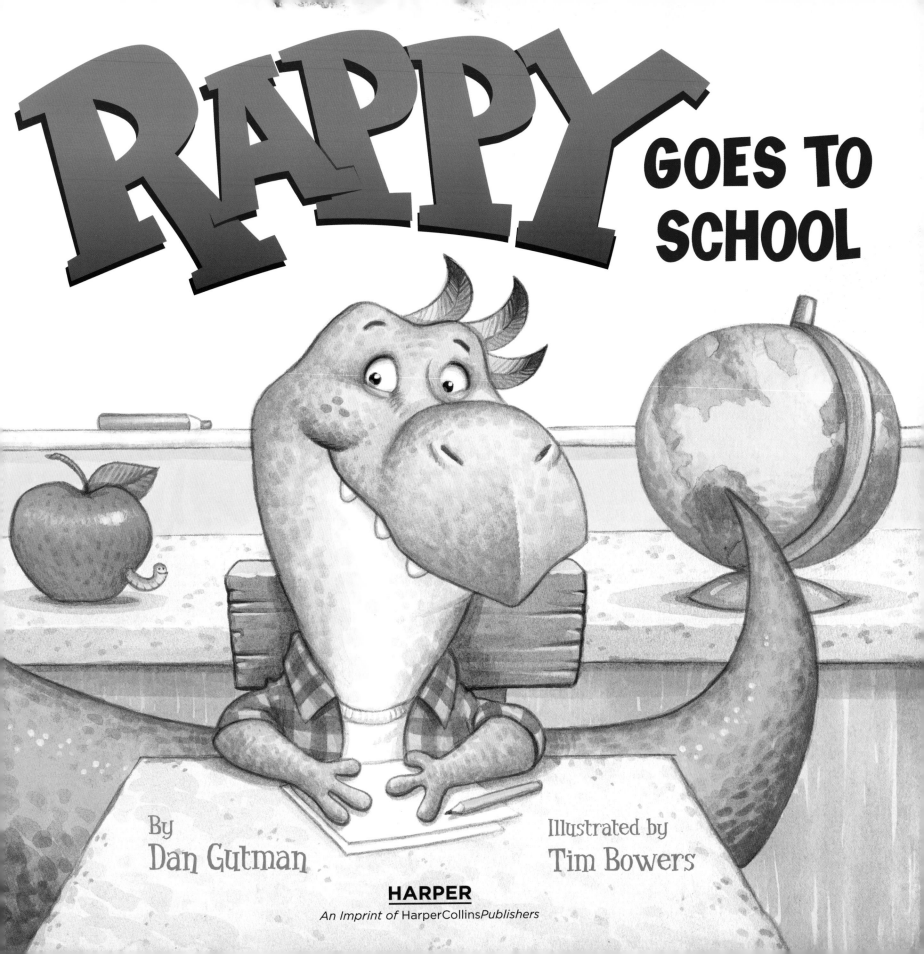

RAPPY GOES TO SCHOOL

By Dan Gutman

Illustrated by Tim Bowers

HARPER

An Imprint of HarperCollinsPublishers

I'm Rappy the Raptor
and I talk in rhyme.
My lyrics are awesome.
Well, most of the time.

What's today's date?
I don't want to be late!
The first day of school
is gonna be cool!

Is it time to go?
Does anyone know?
What do I put my stuff in?
Can I have another muffin?

I gathered up my school supplies.
My sister, Riley, rolled her eyes.

I need pencils and pens.
Do you think I'll make friends?
Will my teacher be kind?
I'm losing my mind!

I feel like a fool.
I don't want to go to school.
Mom said, "Calm down, please!
Stand up straight and say 'cheese!'"

I promised Mom that I'd keep quiet.
She said I might start a riot.
I'm not gonna talk or sing;
I'm not gonna say a thing.

Mrs. Hooperlooper

That's when we first met our teacher,
a huge and terrifying creature!
Her name was Mrs. Hooperlooper.
She told us this year would be super.

Then she had us play a game
where we all had to say our name
and something that we liked to do,
like sing a song or play kazoo.

Judy said she loves to dance.
Alex said he came from France.
Connor wants to fly a jet.
Hannah's gonna be a vet.
Joe and Mia both play soccer.
Niko wants to be a rocker.
Chris just sneered and acted mean.
He looked like he was seventeen.

The last kid, Aidan, he just stared.
I'm pretty sure that he was scared.

"I . . . uh . . . umm . . . well . . . eh . . ."

Chris said Aidan was so lame.

He yelled, "Don't you even know your name?"

That kid Chris is such a jerk.
I hate to sit and watch him smirk.

Aidan's just shy.
Is he gonna cry?
I wish I knew
what I could do.

Wait! I have an idea!

I'm Rappy the Raptor
and I'd like to say
I may not talk in the usual way.
I'm rappin' on the floor,
I'm rappin' when I'm kneeling,
I'm rappin' on the walls,
I'm rappin' on the ceiling.

I'm rappin' in the summer,
I'm rappin' in the fall,
I'm rappin' at the market,
I'm rappin' at the mall.

I'm rappin' at the movies,
I'm rappin' at a play,
I'm rappin' all night,
I'm rappin' all day.

Kids were shouting.

Kids were yelling.

Mrs. H. said, "Time for spelling!"

Oh no! Not that! I'm the worst!

"Rappy, how about you go first?"

I said, "I . . . eh . . . well . . . umm . . . uh . . ."

I couldn't spell *cat*,
I couldn't spell *ring*,
I couldn't spell *bat*,
or anything!
Chris was laughing in my face.
I felt like a big disgrace.

So Aidan told me what to say.
That guy really saved my day.
Cat is spelled C–A–T.
With a *C* and an *A* and a *T–T–T*.
We all agree
cat starts with *C*,
like *can* and *cook* and *cup of tea*.

Then comes *A*,
like *anchors aweigh*,
and *act* and *art* and *all the way*.
Next comes *T*,
like *top* and *three*,
and *tap* and *time* and *Tennessee*.

Mrs. H. held up a card. "Try this one, Rappy; it's not hard."

Dog is spelled D-O-G.

With a *D* and an *O* and a *G-G-G.*

That's the key.

Dog starts with *D,*

like *dark* and *door* and *disagree.*

Then comes *O,*

like *open* and *owe.*

These are words you won't *outgrow.*

Next comes *G,*

like *glad* and *glee,*

and *gap* and *got* and *guarantee.*

We were rappin' all morning.
Rappin' in the halls.
We were rappin' on the tables
and rappin' in the stalls.

We were rappin' at recess
and rappin' at gym.
He was rappin' with me,
and I was rappin' with him.

At three we heard the school bell ring,
and Mrs. H. yelled, "One last thing!"
She said we shouldn't make fun of others,
and if we did she'd tell our mothers.
Being a bully isn't cool,
so she made Chris stay after school!

I'm Rappy the Raptor
and I'd like to say,
I may not talk in the usual way.
I'm rappin' and snappin' all of the time.
I just can't help but talk in rhyme.

Tomorrow I'll go back to school.

Learning stuff is really cool.

Now I know that in the end

all you need is one good friend.